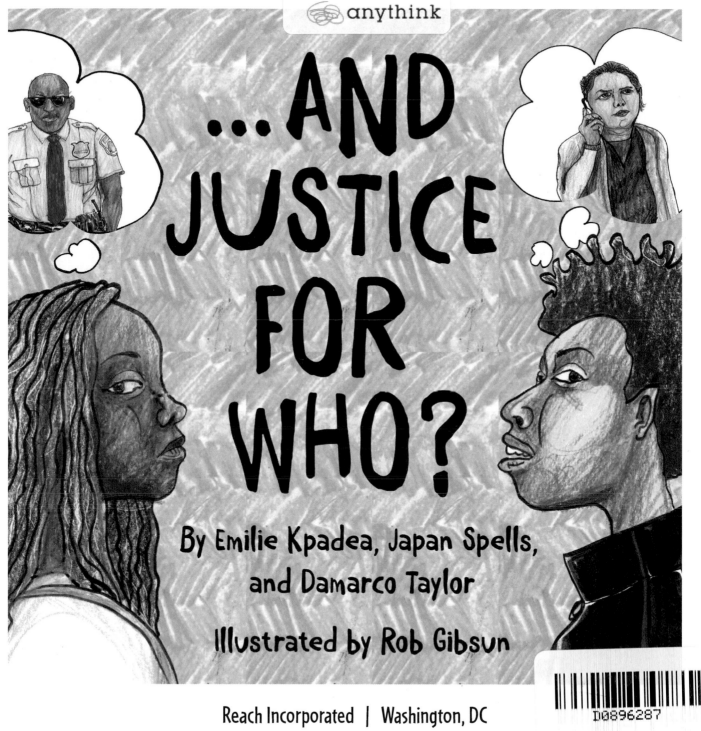

...AND JUSTICE FOR WHO?

By Emilie Kpadea, Japan Spells, and Damarco Taylor

Illustrated by Rob Gibsun

Reach Incorporated | Washington, DC

Shout Mouse Press

Reach Education, Inc. / Shout Mouse Press
Published by
Shout Mouse Press, Inc.

Shout Mouse Press is a nonprofit writing and publishing program dedicated to amplifying underheard voices. This book was produced through Shout Mouse workshops and in collaboration with Shout Mouse artists and editors.

Shout Mouse invites young people from marginalized backgrounds to tell their own stories in their own voices and, as published authors, to act as leaders and agents of change. In partnership with other mission-aligned nonprofits, we are building a catalog of inclusive books that ensure that all children can see themselves represented on the page. Our 300+ authors have produced original children's books, comics, novels, memoirs, and poetry collections.

Learn more and see our full catalog at www.shoutmousepress.org.

Copyright © 2020 Reach Education, Inc.
ISBN-13: 978-1-950807-09-3 (Shout Mouse Press, Inc.)

Special thanks to Anthony White for his art support on this book.

For all the kids learning about injustice.

Cody and Nene are best friends. They have been all their lives.

They hang out and talk about everything.

They have sleepovers and play games together at the park.

They love to ride the swings super high and jump off.

They agree about almost everything...

...until the week of Nene's birthday party.

One sunny afternoon, Cody and Nene leave the school library to walk home. Out front, there's a group of kids scrolling on social media.

Everyone is talking about Black Lives Matter.

There's a video of a police officer talking to a Black man. The officer is mean muggin' and yelling. The Black man on the screen looks worried. Then it gets worse.

Nene is surprised. She thinks about her favorite uncle who is a cop. He's polite and kind to everyone he meets. She hopes he doesn't act like the cop on the video.

Nene says, "Not all cops act like that!"

Cody doesn't say anything. He thinks: *How could someone do such a thing...* Cody feels scared and hopes that he doesn't run into a cop anytime soon... or ever.

The next morning at school, Cody and Nene do the school announcements. They read the Pledge of Allegiance together over the intercom.

While he says the words, Cody starts thinking about the video again.

"...with liberty and justice for all."

Hearing that last line Cody feels confused and overwhelmed. He mumbles: "...and justice for who?"

Cody hears his voice echo through the hallways. His eyes widen. *Did I say that out loud?*

Ms. Wilson, the office assistant, turns off the intercom.

Cody thinks: *Uh oh. What is everybody gonna think?*

When Cody and Nene return to their class, it's awkward in the room. Cody can feel his heart beat fast in his chest.

Some kids huddle together and whisper. They look back at Cody. He feels so nervous!

"All right then, Mr. Black Lives Matter!" Nelson says with a smirk. Some other kids giggle and look away.

At lunch, Cody sits at a table by himself.

Nene comes over and sits down beside him. "Is something wrong?"

Cody shrugs and looks away.

"Hey, we're best friends," says Nene. She leans in close to him. "You can talk to me about anything."

"Well, O.K. It's about this morning. Like when I said, 'and justice for who?' I was saying it's not fair. Cops are out to get us."

Nene leans away. "What do you mean?"

"You seen the news lately? There's protests going on all over the world. Black people get treated differently by police, and that ain't right."

"Well my uncle is a cop, and he treats everyone right."

"You not hearing me! You think what they did to that man was right? Just because your uncle is a cop?"

"I hear you. But you not hearing ME. My uncle is a good cop. There are other good cops, too. It ain't fair that ALL cops are getting blamed! That's just stupid."

Cody picks up his lunch tray, turns his back on Nene, and walks away.

When Cody gets home, his mom is waiting for him in the living room.

She asks, "How was your day, Cody?" But he doesn't respond.

He goes straight to his room and closes the door. He sits down on his bed. He feels so frustrated he could cry. It's the first time he's ever really fought with his best friend. The more he thinks about it, the more he tears up.

Knock, Knock! A few seconds later, his mom walks through the door.

"Cody what's wrong, what's happening?"

"It's nothing."

His mom hugs him around the shoulders. "You can talk to me."

Cody takes a deep breath. "I ain't cool with Nene no more, Ma," he says. "She don't understand me." He looks away. "I don't even know if I wanna go to her birthday party."

"Well," his Mom says. "I'm sorry to hear that. But are you sure you wanna give up on your lifetime best friend? On her birthday? You wanna let one argument break up your friendship?"

Cody doesn't say anything.

That night, after his mom tucks him in, Cody thinks about Nene. Deep down he knows his mom is right. Nene really is his best friend. He already misses talking to her. And he had been so excited for her party tomorrow.

Cody changes his mind. How could he miss his best friend's birthday?

The next day, Cody and his mom go to Nene's birthday party at the park. Cody feels awkward. He's not sure what it'll be like when he sees Nene.

He spots her on the swing. When Nene looks up to see him, her eyes widen in excitement.

Cody says, "Happy birthday!"

"I thought you might not come," Nene says.

Cody doesn't mention the fight. He doesn't want to ruin her birthday.

"I wouldn't miss your party. C'mon, let's play!"

"You know it. I got some new water guns!"

They grab them off the table and go play in the park like they always do.

Nene runs off to hide and Cody chases her. They have so much fun they run past the birthday party and over to the other side of the park, out of sight.

Cody ducks behind a trash can and pops up, trying to catch Nene by surprise. He sees her and raises his water gun to soak her!

All of a sudden, a siren sounds. A police car pulls up and two officers jump out. Nene recognizes one of them. It's Uncle Charles!

"Freeze!" the other officer says to Cody. "Put your hands up where I can see them."

For a second, both Nene and Cody feel scared. What's happening?!

But then Uncle Charles steps in front of them.
"Hold on, hold on! These are kids! I know them.
That's my niece and her friend!"

The other officer relaxes. "Sorry about that. A lady called 911 to report somebody with a gun."

"911? We're just kids playing with water guns," says Nene.

"Why would they call the police on us?" asks Cody.

Uncle Charles gets on his knees and hugs the kids. "That's a good question. A really good question." He looks a little emotional. "I'm just glad you're O.K."

Uncle Charles walks Cody and Nene back to the birthday party. They feel a little shaken up. Their hearts are still racing in their throats.

When they see their friends again, they begin to run. They just want to get back to the party.

After they cut the cake, Cody goes to talk to Uncle Charles.

"Momma always said there's a time and place for everything under the sun. Why is there no time for us to just be kids?"

He smiles, but it's a sad smile. "You're right," he says. "You deserve time to just be kids. I wish I didn't have to tell you to be careful around police officers. Someday I hope I won't."

Cody appreciates hearing that from Uncle Charles. Nene's uncle really is a good man... and a good cop.

The next day at school, Nene and Cody sit together at lunch. They still can't believe what happened to them at the park.

"I'm sorry I didn't believe you before," Nene says. "I get it now. What happened to us was scary, and I know it could have gone different. I can't get it out of my mind."

"I'm sorry too," says Cody. "Your uncle really does try to treat people fairly. I know it's not his fault that Black people don't get treated the same. I'm glad he's trying to make a change in this world, like I want to."

"Me too," says Nene. "Maybe we can go to a protest together? I want to be part of that change."

"Yeahhhhh. Let's get into it!"

About the Authors

Emilie Kpadea

I am Emilie Kpadea, and I am 15 years old. I am a sophomore at Coolidge High School in Washington, DC. I like playing sports, writing, baking, and cooking. This is my first book. I wrote this book because in this world there is a lot of injustice against African Americans, and letting kids learn about this through story is a good way to spread the word and get them talking.

Japan Spells

My name is Japan Spells, and I'm a junior at Anacostia High School in Washington, DC. I am captain of our Anacostia cheerleading team. This is my second book with Reach and Shout Mouse; last year I co-wrote *Game of Pharaohs* (2019). I wrote this book to portray real acts of injustice while also showing that all cops are not bad. The problem is bigger than individuals. Just getting kids to understand that at a young age is powerful.

Damarco Taylor

My name is Damarco Taylor and I'm a 17-year-old senior at Luke C. Moore High School in Washington, DC. I enjoy basketball and making clothing. I'll be dropping a new clothing line soon, and I hope you'll check it out! This is my first book. I hope that this story will provide all our readers some understanding of the impact of police violence.

Faith Campbell served as Story Coach for this book.

Hayes Davis served as Head Story Coach for this year's series.

About the Illustrator

Rob Gibson

Born in Richmond, Virginia, Rob Gibson has been in love with the visual and performing arts since his youth. He is a graduate of Virginia Commonwealth University's Communication Arts department and is the founder of VCU's award-winning poetry organization, "Good Clear Sound." Rob's art and poetry have been published in Yemassee Journal, The Offing, Kinfolks Quarterly, Minetta Review, and Amendment. As a teaching artist, a TEDxRVA Speaker, a Southern Fried Poetry Slam Champion, and a Verses and Flow Poet, he urges you to keep it real, create fearlessly, and work with what you got to get what you want. Find more of Rob's art at robartistic.weebly.com.

Writers and artists at work

Acknowledgments

For the eighth summer in a row, teens from Reach Incorporated were issued a challenge: compose original children's books that will both educate and entertain young readers. Specifically, these teens were asked to create inclusive stories that reflect their lived experiences – experiences that this year include the current global pandemic and the struggle for racial justice. As always, these teens have demonstrated that they know their audience, they believe in their mission, and they take pride in the impact they can make on young lives.

Thirteen writers spent the month of July brainstorming ideas, generating potential plots, writing, revising, and providing critiques. Authoring quality books is challenging work at any time, but this year, these young people had to collaborate virtually, during a COVID-19 shutdown. These authors have our immense gratitude and respect: Jocktavious, Daveena, Geralyn, Shatyia, Japan, Damarco, Emilie, Riley, Anthony, Diarou, Danya, Joseph, and Samaria.

These books represent a collaboration between Reach Incorporated and Shout Mouse Press, and we are grateful for the leadership provided by members of both teams. From Reach, Anyssa Dhaouadi, Victoria Feathersone, and Charles Walker contributed meaningfully to discussions and morale, and the Reach summer program leadership of Jusna Perrin kept us organized and connected, even while we all worked apart. From the Shout Mouse Press team, we thank Head Story Coach Hayes Davis, who oversaw this year's workshops, and Story Coaches Barrett Smith, Sarai Johnson, Faith Campbell, and Alexa Patrick for bringing both fun and insight to the project. We can't thank enough illustrators Camryn Simms, Anthony White, Alex Perkins, and Rob Gibson for bringing these stories to life with their beautiful artwork. Finally, Amber Colleran brought a keen eye and important mentorship to the project as the series Art Director and book designer. We are grateful for the time and talents of these writers and artists!

Finally, we thank those of you who have purchased books and cheered on our authors. It is your support that makes it possible for these teen authors to engage and inspire young readers. We hope you smile as much while you read as these teens did while they wrote.

Mark Hecker,
Reach Incorporated

Kathy Crutcher,
Shout Mouse Press

About Reach Incorporated

Reach

Reach Incorporated develops readers and leaders by preparing teens to serve as tutors and role models for younger students, resulting in improved literacy outcomes for both the teen tutors and their elementary school students.

Founded in 2009, Reach recruits high school students to be elementary school reading tutors. After completing a year in our program, teens gain access to additional leadership development opportunities, including The Summer Leadership Academy and The College Mentorship Program. All of this exists within our unique college and career preparation framework, The Reach Fellowship. Through this comprehensive system of supports, teens are prepared to thrive in high school and beyond.

Through their work as reading tutors, our teens noticed that the books they read with their students did not always reflect their lived experiences. As always, we felt the best way we could address this issue was to put our teens in charge. Through our collaboration with Shout Mouse Press, these teens create engaging stories with diverse characters that invite young readers to explore the world through words. By purchasing our books, you support student-led, community-driven efforts to improve educational outcomes in the District of Columbia.

Learn more at www.reachincorporated.org.

Made in the USA
Monee, IL
09 December 2020

5203449R00024